My Mom Is Going Back to School

by Debbie Cavalier

Illustrated by Dana Regan

Dedicated to all the moms and dads who sacrifice so much in order to pursue their education and make a better life for their families. You are an inspiration!

–D.C.

Editor: Jonathan Feist

ISBN 978-0-578-50013-3
Printed in the United States of America

Hi, I'm Bryce. I'm 8 years old, and I play on my soccer team.

I have a mom and a dad, a sister, and a cat, and I LOVE to eat ice cream!

Today, I learned some news. My mom is going back to school!

She wants to learn new skills, earn her degree, and get a new job one day.

Dad says things will be different. We'll need to help out along the way.

Mom'll need time to study, and she'll have less time to play.

I understand and I'll lend a hand, even help with my baby sister, Jane.

I think it's just so cool that Mom and I will both be in school!

I can't wait till we're study buddies! We'll do our homework together
every night.

And we'll talk about our teachers and the friends we made in person and online.

We'll pack our lunch in the mornings, and set out on our way.

I'll go to school and Mom'll go to work, then some classes at the end of her day.

We'll both bring home report cards, and proudly hang them on the fridge.

We'll get good grades, and if you covered the names, you wouldn't know which is which!

We'll celebrate our progress with ice cream, 'cause ice cream is the best!

Then it's bedtime for me and my family, but Mom will have to study for her test.

And before we know it, graduation day will be here! We'll watch Mom receive her diploma, and we'll clap, and we'll yell, and we'll cheer!

Mom in her cap and gown, she'll look like a queen with a crown! Then we'll celebrate with an ice cream cake. It will be the best day of the year!

I'm proud of my mom, and she's proud of me.

We're a lifelong learning family!

What's that? Dad has some news? "Yes, I'm going back to school, too!"
Hurray!!!

Draw a picture of your mom wearing her graduation hat.

Write your mom's name and the name of her school on the diploma.